Pip Stories

Written and Illustrated

by LEON STEINMETZ

Little, Brown and Company

BOSTON   TORONTO

To Fram

COPYRIGHT © 1980 BY LEON STEINMETZ

Library of Congress Cataloging in Publication Data

Steinmetz, Leon.
  Pip stories.

  SUMMARY: In four separate adventures, an energetic porcupine tries to fly, reach the moon, become famous, and find the sun.
  [1. Porcupines—Fiction] I. Title.
PZ7.S8277PO   [E]   78–15061
ISBN 0–316–78738–8

FIRST EDITION

H
*Published simultaneously in Canada
by Little, Brown & Company (Canada) Limited*

PRINTED IN THE UNITED STATES OF AMERICA

How Pip Tried to Fly

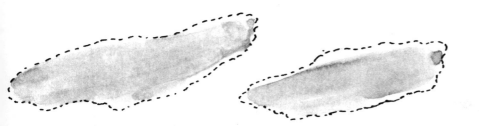

"How nice to fly!" thought Pip Porcupine.

"Up high you can see everything.

You can fly over the woods.

If there isn't a bridge,

You can fly over the river.

You can fly over mountains.

I will ask somebody

who can fly

how to do it."

He called to a little dragonfly:

"Dragonfly, tell me

what I need to fly."

"You have to be light,"

said the dragonfly and flew away.

"That's easy,"

Pip said to himself.

"I'm very light."

He jumped up, but he came down.

"I can jump high,

but I can't fly.

To be light is not enough.

I need something else."

He saw a young crow sitting in a tree.

"Tell me, Crow,

what I need to fly,"

Pip asked.

"You need wings," said the crow.

He spread his wings and glided away.

"I see," said Pip.

"It's easy to make wings."

9

He picked two big leaves

and held them in his paws.

He stretched his paws out wide.

"Now I will fly," he thought.

He waited and waited

with his paws spread wide

but he didn't fly.

"No, I need something else,"

he said.

He looked up

and saw a small butterfly.

"Hey, Butterfly,

what do I need to fly?"

Pip shouted.

"You must flap, flap, flap your wings very fast,"

cried the butterfly,

and kept on flying.

"I can do that,"

Pip said.

"Now I know *everything*

about flying.

I will climb high in a tree

and fly like the birds."

Pip climbed a tree.

He jumped high,

flapped his wings and flew.

But he did not fly up.

He flew head first to the ground.

Good thing that he landed

in a pile of dried leaves!

13

He crawled out of the leaves,

and shook himself off.

He thought about the dragonfly,

the crow and the butterfly.

"Now I know why I can't fly,"

he said to himself.

"You can only learn to fly

when you are a baby.

After that,

it is too late."

How Pip Tried to Reach the Moon

Pip sat by his hole

and looked at the moon.

The moon was very near.

It hung right over the woods.

"It must be nice on the moon,"

Pip thought.

"But I don't know how to get there,"

he said to himself.

17

At that moment the sly coyote came by.

"Did you say something to me?"

asked the coyote.

"No, I was just talking to myself,"

said Pip.

"And what did you say to yourself?"

asked the coyote.

"I said, how nice to be on the moon,"

said Pip.

18

"Well, I can help you to get there,"

said the coyote, laughing.

"Why are you laughing, Coyote?"

asked Pip.

"I am laughing for joy,"

said the coyote.

"I can imagine how you

will go to the moon,

and wave to me from there."

"I will not only wave to you,
I will also bring you something
from the moon.
Only tell me how to get there,"
Pip said.

"Do you see the moonlight

on the ground?"

said the coyote.

"Just stand on it,

turn your face to the moon,

then count to three,

close your eyes,

and run straight ahead

without stopping.

When you see stars in your eyes,

you will know how close a porcupine

can get to the moon."

Pip stood on the patch of moonlight,

turned his face to the moon,

counted to three,

closed his eyes,

and ran as fast as he could.

22

Suddenly something hit him on the nose

so hard

that stars danced before his eyes.

Pip looked . . .

He was standing with his nose

against a big tree.

The moon was still hanging

over the woods.

And the coyote was laughing.

"Now you see how close

a porcupine can get to

the moon," he said.

How Pip Tried to Be Famous

ow wonderful to be famous!"

Pip said to himself.

"If you are famous

everyone knows you.

If you are famous

everyone loves you.

How can I be famous?"

he asked himself.

"I know!

I will discover unknown lands.

For that I must be a sailor like Columbus.

But where can I get a ship?"

Pip thought and thought

and had an idea.

In the woods

he found some fallen trees

and dragged them

to the bank of the pond.

He broke off all the branches.

He braided rope from grass.

He tied the trunks together

with the rope

and made a raft.

Then he pushed his ship into the water.

29

"Oh, I almost forgot

the most important thing!"

he said.

He took a stick

and stuck it in the ground.

He tied a piece of bark to it,

and wrote on the bark:

From this place
the Great Sailor Pip
Began His Voyage.

He climbed onto the raft

and got ready to sail.

At that moment

a family of beavers

came to the bank.

"Where are you going, Pip?"

asked the papa beaver.

"To discover unknown lands,"

said Pip.

"But this is a pond," said the mama beaver.

"So what?" said Pip.

"From a pond you can't get anywhere,"

said the beavers in a chorus.

"Why? Isn't this water?"

asked Pip.

"Yes, it is," said the beavers.

"And water, you see, always

comes from somewhere

and goes to somewhere different,"

said Pip.

"So this water

must go somewhere different too."

"But water stays in a pond,"

said the papa beaver.

"That can't be,"

said Pip.

"Goodbye. I will discover new lands.

I am like Columbus."

He waved

and sailed off on the raft.

"I will sail along the bank," he decided.

"When I see unknown mountains or deserts, then I will stop."

Pip sailed along the bank

for an hour.

But on the shore

he saw the woods that he knew.

He sailed for two hours.

The same woods were on the bank.

He sailed for three hours.

There were no mountains

and no deserts.

He sailed a little more and saw . . .

a stick standing on the bank.

A piece of bark

was tied to the stick.

Pip sailed closer and read:

From this place
the Great Sailor Pip
Began His Voyage.

"How can this be?"

Pip thought.

He stood by the stick

and suddenly heard:

36

"Ha-ha-ha, Hee-hee-hee!

Welcome to the unknown land, Columbus!"

Pip looked

and saw the beaver family.

They laughed so hard at him,

and they all fell to the ground.

"There is nothing to laugh about,"

said Pip.

"I just sailed in the wrong direction.

Next time I *will* find a new land.

I will sail the opposite way."

38

"It will soon be winter," thought Pip.

"It will get cold.

I have to do something

to warm up my hole in the winter.

What can I do?

I know!" he cried.

"Every evening the sun sets behind the woods.

I will go to the place where it sets

and break off a piece of the sun.

I will put this piece in my hole.

Then it will always be warm there. . . .

What a good idea I have!

What a fine fellow I am!"

That evening he climbed a tree
to see exactly where
the sun set.

"Very good,"

he said to himself,

"the sun sets behind a big oak

on the edge of the woods."

42

The next day

Pip went to the big oak.

He waited.

Evening came.

The sun started to set.

And Pip saw

that the sun

did not set behind the oak.

It set far away

on the edge of the field.

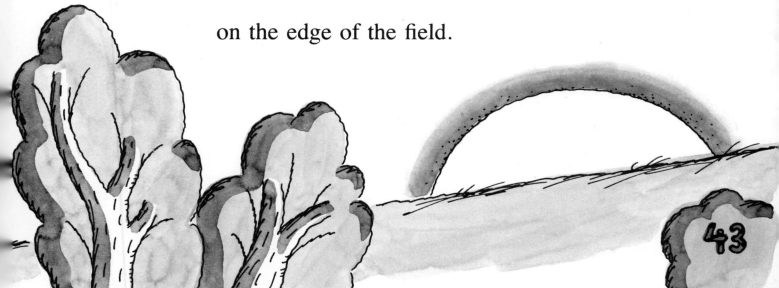

Pip went

to the edge of the field.

But the sun wasn't there either.

It set further,

behind the mountain.

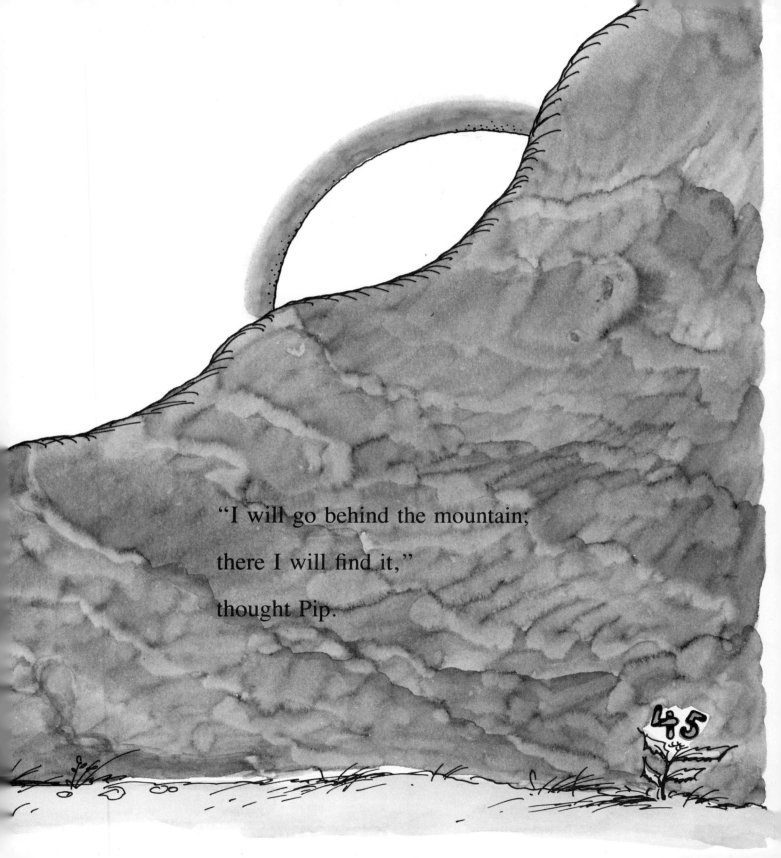

"I will go behind the mountain;

there I will find it,"

thought Pip.

45

He walked along the road

and met three little foxes.

They were brothers.

"Where are you going, Pip?" asked the brothers.

"I won't tell you,

or you will go there too

and there won't be enough for me,"

said Pip.

"We won't go," said the foxes.

"We're going the other way

to visit our aunt."

"Well, all right, I will tell you. . . .

I'm going after the sun,"

said Pip.

"After the sun?" said the foxes.
"Yes. I want to go
to the place where the sun sets
and break off a piece of the sun.
It will warm my hole all winter!"
Pip said proudly.
"But there is no such place,"
the foxes said.
"The sun doesn't set anywhere.
It's the earth that turns
and it only seems
that the sun sets."
"Oh, no! No! It can't be!"
Pip said.

"I will find this place.

And you will see

that *I* am right!"

and he ran, and ran, and ran . . .

down the road

toward the place where

the sun sets.

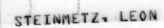